THE WORLD OF

Cover artwork by Karolina Urbánková

By the same author:

Dark Corners of Prague

Horror Story

Life's Kills

The Monster of Draždiak and Other Stories

CONTENTS

ABYSSMAL

There's a cordoned-off section of town
Where someone's dug a car-sized hole in the ground
Shopping gossipers stop and stare
But no-one seems to know why it's there

I'm sure I'm not who I'm meant to be
The person presented is not the real me
The cupboard is empty, pantry is bare
Please spare a thought for the thoughts gone spare

There's a gaping gulf in my theory
A yawning flaw in my plot
I'm an empty vessel full of myself
A little is my lot

(We look to the heavens
Using a telescope
To put the void
Under the microscope)

I sit, fit, and stare into space
MIND THE GAP emblazoned on my face
Millions spent to study black holes
Yet Earth hosts billions of our souls

AT DAGGERS DRAWN

Why do so many who've been abused
End up becoming abusers?
So many victims of oppression
Become tyranny's next in succession?
Why does Israel do
What it does in Palestine?
Wherever in history was the starting line?
Surely what we're doing in the present
Is that by which we're most accurately defined?

Sometimes a people
We'll call them people A
Oppress a people B
And the balance of power is flipped
As we might have seen
With Babylonia and Assyria
Tutsis and Hutus
Manchu and Han
Sometimes tit for tat
Is about rights and recognition
Russians and Lithuanians
Hungarians and Transylvanians
Anglophone and Francophone signage in Quebec
I mean, what the heck?
Profoundly protracted playground squabbles
Have civilisation by the neck

Amoral greed
Needs to create a need
For conflict
Resentment, entitlement
Bloodlust dressed as just cause
The arms trade the only winner
Of well-lobbied laws and well-oiled wars

You need to cultivate hate
To dominate
Make the rules cruel
Keep animosity's fires fuelled
Have each side thinking they're the have-nots
To amass your unappreciated ill-gotten lot
It's not a state secret
Or matter of national security
The more compassionate
We're encouraged to be
The less the power-hungry
Have authority

AUSCHWITZ

We pulled up in the parking lot
Designed for visitors
Or tourists
The lot was full of cars
That had arrived full of people
Uncomfortable or unable
To think of themselves
As visitors or tourists
We were here to learn
Of a past that can never be repeated
Or the history lesson
That the idea we can learn from history
Is an idea itself by history defeated

We were conscious of effecting
A suitably sombre air
Of the expressions on our faces
Our postures and paces
As we made our voluntary way
To the gate through which countless
Were marched across the threshold
Without a prayer
Able to do little beyond pray

The four of us
Were nazis
Or, rather, the neo-Nazis' version thereof
Now that neo-Nazis
Accuse you of being a nazi
For picking them up
On having the opinions of Nazism
Hell, I was even a grammar nazi
Beneath the wrought iron sign we passed
Before it was stolen, replaced with a replica, then
retrieved and relocated to a museum display
The B in ARBEIT
Forged by camp inmates
Inverted
Fondly regarded
As an act of defiance
Trivial
Or of consequential magnitude
Who gets to say?

For all the unthinkable horrors
The atmosphere
Was somehow...somehow...
Somehow not blanketed with horror
I did not even feel it
Saturated with grief
Instead, a peculiar numbness
As if 200 hectares
Had had all the emotion ripped away
Had been stripped of feeling
To protect the sanity
Or maybe that was just some self-preservation
Going on in my brain

These Polish army barracks
Cum benchmark for everything
With humanity that is wrong
Is 28 brick blocks
With maintained integrity
If one did not know where one was
It would hardly appear reminiscent
Of archetypal torture chamber imagery
For all the depravity and heinousness
To the exteriors, there is a certain innocuousness
But maybe just as the darkest minds
Lurk behind suits and ties
And keep to the legal side of the lines
A somehow normalisation to the abomination
Somehow becomes part of the place and time

We pored over the
Artefacts and displays
With studious deliberation
Then gradually hastened our step
Glossing over
The footprints of genocide
The way one hears of
Another US school shooting
Shrugging at mass deaths
Mumbling 'That's life.'

Even death
Even torture
Even extermination
Even Eichmann's final solution
Become pedestrian and routine after a while
Were it to work any other way
Would this place
And the part of our past it symbolises
Ever have been made manifest?
Would the unspeakable ever get to have its say?

Block 10
A Frankensteinian laboratory
Children, women and men
Forcibly subjected to alleged medical
    experimentation
Of the test subjects, a chief buyer
Was Bayer

Block 11
"The Block of Death"
With its makeshift court
The wall
In the adjoining yard
Pockmarked
With hole after hole

The other side of vast panes of glass
Are eyeglasses after eyeglasses
Spectacles
Pince-nez
Monocles
It's hard to tear the gaze away

Artificial limbs
Prosthetic devices
Confiscated
Discarded
Stolen by the heartless

The children's toys
How many children's toys
Were taken from how many hands
Of how many children
Crying how many tears?

Several visitors paused to take selfies
Some wearing smiles
One man stood posing
Legs apart
Both hands held
As if holding
A ZB-26
I wonder how many likes that got?

The gas chamber
Was just one side of the perimeter fence
Residential housing just the other
I had been told
The stench of death
Lingered in its confines
I wondered what
A Holocaust denier might smell
But I'm not sure one has ever visited the place
And gone on to tell such a tale

Our group regrouped
After having become separated
Where once people were segregated
By armbands announcing
Trade unionist
Homosexual
Gypsy
Jew

'Are we doing Birkenau as well?'
I found myself asking
With all the sensitivity, tact and absent-mindedness
Of my own self-styled lost generation

On the three-kilometre drive
Between the camps
Upon clocking the plates
Of our foreign rental car
A young boy wearing glasses
Threw stones at the windows
As we went past

The unpretentiously dubbed death camp
Now a largely open field
With traces of the foundations
Where its wooden blocks used to stand
Some remain
Looking like farmyard barns
From which the animals have been cleaned out
'What are those?' one of our party asked
'They're latrines,' I replied
Though the word sounded too French and sanitary
'Don't be silly.
People didn't use those as a toilet.'
'Oh yes,' I said,
'They did.'

We wandered around the grounds
Seeing what there was left to see
Which was nothing much left to see
We felt it our duty to linger longer
Especially knowing many were forced to remain
    here
The rest of their lives
Including, I felt certain
Most of the very few who left here alive

The other side of the street
From the camp
Stood a church
Its bells pealing
Its doors opened
People started spilling out
Our eyes opened wide
Here came a groom and
Here comes the bride
What?
Here, across the road from the camp
A couple had tied the knot
I kid you not
I didn't know what to think about it
I didn't know what I was meant to think about it
I didn't know what was the decent thing to think
Life goes on, no matter what

We left the town
And headed for Kraków
Then later returned to Prague
Leaving the past behind
Entering a future
In which Uyghur re-education
Kadyrov's purge
The ethnocide of Tatars
And the Harris Ranch
Would barely make headlines

BETWEEN YOU AND ME, I'VE A THEORY ABOUT CONSPIRACY THEORIES

A plan to achieve something unlawful
Something awful
A plan to deceive
Something nefarious up the sleeve
Harmful, detrimental
Secretly experimental
Almost always causing hurt
All of us always a little alert

There are those who suggest they've their feet on the
   ground
Which apparently implies their mind is sound
I think of all the times mine has let me down
Perhaps I'm plotting against myself
Well, what goes round comes around

Some people believe in the ridiculous
The frankly idiotically ludicrous
Some notions folk entertain
Are arguably insane
We are presided over
By shape-shifting aliens
They might look like people
But they're actually 'reptilians'
It might be *très* out there but it sounds kind of cool
When Carpenter brought *They Live* to life
He seemed to think so too

Apollo 11
Did your eyes just roll toward heaven?
I personally take my hat off to those for whom
    nothing's a given
The science and the scepticism
Allegedly yawning holes
From either side yawningly told
Hard to believe a mission to the moon's provable fact
When I can't get up from the keyboard in my squalid
    flat

Conspiracy theorists are naïve
Are paranoid
Are mentally ill
Have probably skipped their pills
Yes, we mean it derogatorily
But kind of light-heartedly
Yet also semi-seriously
See, nobody quite knows what they do and don't
Or what they would or would not like to believe
Fanaticism is rage against doubt
Keep your options open, kindly leave the smugness
    out

The minimum number of conspirators required
To forge a conspiracy
Totals one less than three
Politically
Corporately
Extra-maritally
From children to the retired
The well-connected to the unplugged haywired
Everyone's at it or is subjected to it
One way or the other
By their MP, supervisor, lover, or their mother

Films
Books
Legends
History
Sketches
Skits
Myths
Cartoons
Stories in general
Have conspiracy as an integral part of their plot
Think about it, make a list
How many tales tell of conspiracies
And how many do not?

Anyone who goes to church
Believes in one of the most prevailing conspiracy
    theories of all
In which we are the conspirators
You can scoff at truthers all you like
Truth conspires against us by hiding in plain sight

When conspiracy theorists are presented
As nutjobs
Unicorn hunters
Flat Earthers
Holocaust deniers
Might this not be
In itself a conspiracy
To dissuade people from investigating
How the mechanisms of geopolitics
And the wheels of the system with all its tricks
Really tick?
Keep us under semi-veiled tyranny?
Now you're looking at me with a peculiar expression
    on your face
Wait a minute! Is that dry skin or scales?
Are you really of the human race??

Surely the majority of conspiracy theories
Are harmless fun
And others deal with brevity
Like 911
Tell me, are you a legitimate expert
On aeronautics,
Pyrotechnics,
Construction,
National defense,
Film analysis
Plus are you, especially with yourself, brutally
    honest?
No-one is the top dog on all the above
A plane seemingly melting into the tower's *façade*?
The official line's in itself a conspiracy theory – isn't
    that mad?
If I said I'm not a sceptic, I'd be lying
I've tried to make sense of it, but succeeded only in
    trying

You might not want to think of yourself as a
    conspiracy theorist
Or certainly be labelled as such
You might even feel more comfortable with being
    called a terrorist
But the fact is, the bottom line
A theorist about conspiracies
Is what you are
If your senses are intact
And that, though squirm and seethe you might
Is an incontrovertible fact
If that's something you refute, if it makes you angry
You'll have to change the meanings of 'conspiracy'
    and of 'theory'
Maybe 'paranoid theorist' would be a more
    appropriate term
For those who believe nanobots can be injected like
    sperm

And by the way, if the Titanic was sunk
By an enormous floating ice chunk
When the wreckage was found beneath the sea
How come no 'berg was there? How could that be??

And shampoo seems to contain
Substances that can manipulate your brain
Of alien abductions, it seems the most aware
Are those who forego washing their hair

And the PC
Extinction Rebellion
BLM
The LGBT
Are all in it together, see?
Along with the Muslims and the reds
Conspiring to prevent
Decent church-going semi-literate white
    conservatives
From shooting each other with their private arsenals
And taking their cousins to bed

Anyway, I have to run now
I'm being monitored
They're after me, you see?
I read about it on Facebook
And Twitter, Breitbart
And QAnon told me
They say that I'm a bigot
But my mum assures me I'm nice
But let's keep it down to a whisper
Alexa, can you sweep for a bugging device?

BEWARE OF THE DOG

In the 16th century
The Chinese
Popularised themselves
Among royalty
Beyond their own
Imperial dynasty
In many a land
And territory

The Industrial Revolution
Caused Englanders
To cross the Channel
And relocate to France
Endearing themselves
They came to be known
As French themselves
In common parlance

During World War Two
In concentration camps
As guards and terrorisers
Germans were employed
Their intelligence so high
They're allied with police
And in search and rescue missions
Are commonly deployed

Many a Chihuahuan
Has crossed the border
From Mexico to the States
No-one barking orders
No-one shouting words of hate

Afghans
Walk the streets of London
No fear of accusation
Of being terrorists
Or, even worse
Having refugee status

When Sarajevo was under
A three-year siege
A Tornjak ran
Through the streets of Belgrade
Sniffing at
A Sarplaninac
Its hindquarters
Undefensively displayed

A Turkish boy in Cyprus
Takes his Molosser
To faithfully keep pace
On his morning run
A few streets away
An aged Greek lady
Laughs as her Koyun
Steals crumbs from her bun

A Slovak plays
With his Wirehaired Vizsla
'Fore venturing out
To the Danube for a stroll
Listening to the happy
Yap of the Cuvac
Of Mr Meszaros
In the apartment below

Who respects
Nationalities?
Countries?
Races?
Histories?
Cultures?
And wars?
Man does
And entitlement and riches
And those who have none
For the above
Are sons of bitches

Who could need more
When he's his own worst enemy
Than one he calls his best friend
And, leashed by the past
Cannot see past
His own dry nose's end?

BONDAGE

There must be plenty of men
In a penitentiary
In solitary
Under suicide watch
Who can never be free of knowing
They'll never be free

There are countless
Literally countless
Meaning you can't count them
And nobody else is going to either
Sleeping beneath the stars
Or the feeble shelter afforded
For those who can only afford
A shop doorway
They don't have to make mortgage repayments
Or worry how they're going to
Like countless with a roof over their head do

And what about nuclear families
In which children lack reaction
When craving a parent's attention
In which a member is having a meltdown
Reeling in the feelings at their core
Lest they all suffer the fallout
Of a half-life or more

Bosses
Must answer to their own bosses
Their own bosses
Must answer to their wives
Their wives
Must answer to their peers
Their peers
Must answer to their stifled, hidden tears

Dictators
Must distrust in order to survive
Must kill more and more
In order their version of order thrives
Must get edgier and edgier
Ever dreading
The edge of the retributive knife

The humble
Those who enjoy, if not a myth
A simple lifestyle
Do they fear a bureaucratic tangle
Or love triangle
Or circumstance in earnest
Of rendering their carefree existence erstwhile?

Is staying youthful
At odds or in tune with staying truthful?
Is it possible to be adored
And then, when it suits you, be ignored?
Oh, to be a musician millions revere
But oh, to play a hundred-plus gigs a year
Oh, to be a Tinseltown top-billing actor
But oh, to be ambassador for corporate sponsors
Would you rather quietly have it all
Or have it written on the wall?
Would you rather have everyone you do
Or don't like be enviously awed?

The fingers on the buttons
Are on hands that are tied
The Walk of Fame handprints
Have Weinstein alongside
From Aramazd to Zeus
All are compromised
Who wouldn't want a day off
Of being deified?

If you take yourself somewhere
Without asking or telling a soul
Someplace nobody can disturb or observe you
Having left the phone at home
And sit down and open a book
And lose yourself in the page
Are you giving yourself the illusion of freedom
Or seeing the world's in an illusory cage?

THE CAUSE

Nuclear missiles are flying again
Pollutants pepper the breeze
Species are on the brink of extinction
Healthcare's on its knees
The welfare state's in tatters
Deficit's an abyss
War crimes are abundant
Humanity is amiss

Fascism's now in fashion
Racism's all the rage
Damn, my bookmark's fallen out
I've been and lost the page
Genocide's back with a vengeance
Nationalism's the norm
And my shoes won't last the season
The soles look good and worn

Corruption is epidemic
The world is run by fools
Our grandchildren are damned
It's time to hit the booze
There must be something I can do
To help the poor and meek
There must be something I can do
To fix that goddamn leak

There's a refugee crisis
People are forced to beg
He can't feed his children
She's homeless without legs
There's a shortfall for the pensions
And I'm almost out of cash
And I'm almost out of patience
And I'm almost out of hash

The seas are choked with plastic
Topsoil's all but gone
And today's a bloody meeting
That'll go on and on and on
My partner doesn't treat me right
It's like I don't exist
I need to see the doctor
Not sure this is a cyst

The landlord won't be happy
The rent is late again
I can't shift this headache
Or get rid of that stain
When the hell's her birthday?
Or due date for that loan?
Christ, I need to get a life
Replace this stupid phone

I believe in fighting the good fight
I believe in battling for what's right
And as soon as I've taken care of this nonsense
I'll...

CHARLES WASN'T THE FIRST

How many times have you heard someone say
'I would never...'
In an unsolicited way
And believed them?
Have you ever?

How many times
'If it had been me...'
And considered them heroic
Seriously?

How many pictures, faces and names
On posters, tattoos and tees
Slipped into shame
And laser-removed memory?

How many times
'This is the one, I know it's the one.'
Can you count
Before you include your thumb?

How many times did
'You don't have the right to comment on...'
'You don't know what you're talking about.'
Make someone nod and say,
'Thank you for showing me the error of my ways.'?

How many times
Have those you voted for
Let you down?
What looked like fun, thrills, laughs
Turn to tears, sneers, frowns?

How much rebellion sold out?
Vintage wine turned sour?
How much hope and integrity
Got sidelined,
Corrupted,
Or just watered down
By power?

The party faithful can turn their coats
Born leaders get left behind
Gentlemen can make sexist remarks
Women can change their bloody minds

But just as the early bird
Can turn up late
A surprisingly sunny day
Can hand the weatherman his butt on a plate

The role is not the actor
The artist is not the art
Salvador dallied with Francoism
And yet his clocks melted hearts

Imagine eating a killer quiche Lorraine
Made by the same cook
Who then prepared you coffee
Like something you'd use to clean a drain

Respectably or not
We respect
Admirably or otherwise
We admire
Whatever our values
We see ours as above
Conditioned or conditionally
We love

But put a person, thing or place
And especially your own name and face
Up on a pedestal
One way or another
One day or the other
Gravity will make you look a fool

THE COMPASS OF EVIL

A girl on the bus
Young, in her prime
Her head shaved on one side
Exposing a tattoo
The logo of the SS
Unmistakable, clear
Jagged, angular, lightning-like
Unselfconsciously displayed
Conscientiously paraded
Shares a joke with
A man in the seat beside her
His arm wrapped around her
He notices me noticing
In his eyes, a flare
Daring me to say something
I turn my gaze
Back to the backs of heads
Of fellow passengers
Shepherded strangers
None of them talking
The silent majority
Me among their ranks

The security guard
At the casino
Hulking, imposing, thick of neck
But not quite strong enough to protect people from
    entering
Laughs as he hears
The story on the news
On the TV above the bar
A farm has suffered a massive fire
A blazing inferno has consumed its barns
Hundreds of animals burned to a possibly merciful
    death
He imagines how they sounded
He bleats, moos, squeals
In a way only he seems to deem comic
But none of his colleagues pick him up on it
He wonders if the firefighters
Considered the smell of bacon
A perk of the job
I don't think I'll ever forget him
And I've remembered him especially
The times I've eaten pork

Two men locked in argument
Increasingly overheated
Alcohol- and adrenaline-fuelled
Clearly familiar
For as long as it has taken for contempt to be bred
One a wiry weasel
Fractured of ego, broken of tooth
Shouts at the other
An elderly man with a white cane
Over and over again
'Blind cunt!' he snarls
'Blind cunt!' he spits
Clearly comfortable no-one that matters can see or
    hear
He looks pleased with himself
As he repeats it over and over
Onlookers appear too horrified
To do a thing but stop and blink
And the aggressor picks up a bottle beside him
Rewarding himself with a drink

THE DARK TRIAD TRAITS

Someone
Thirty-something
Employed as an IT-something
Scrolls his well-fed finger
Up and down his fat phone screen
A fluctuating fraction
Of his attention
On the conversation
He interrupts
With a contribution
The declaration
The beaches of Europe
Would best be served
By garrisons deployed
So the displaced are destroyed
Who dare to try
To flee the fate
He decrees
They deserve
His shot fired
His voice fizzles out
Something has appeared
On his mobile display
Stealing back his focus
Clearly losing interest
In those he has condemned
To a watery grave

A TV drama
From decades past
Digitalised
And preserved
Uploaded to YouTube
For old and new
Generations to enjoy
Appreciated
Or ill-deserved
Thank you, comes a comment
For the nostalgia trip
A welcome stroll
Down memory lane
Similar messages
Juxtapose crudely
With one prosaic
Needless and profane
The lead actress
One lusts to introduce
To his carnal intentions
Against her will
His electronic footprint
Leaving an indelible
Stain, perhaps fuelling
Whatever frisson
Such iniquity
Afforded him, still

The Mexican/Arizonian border
A fine line between dead and alive
An area known as The Graveyard
A crossing point for many
Minus documents
But raging thirst
In lieu of a green card
Outpost guards
On sandy US turf
Discover bottled water
Left by volunteers
Aware of the hundreds
Who succumb to dehydration
And la muerte
Every single year
Despite the cameras
Or maybe because
They empty the contents
Onto the ground
Then kick the bottles into the air
Littering the surrounds
Jeering and laughing
They swagger away
Mission accomplished
They resume their patrol
Turning their back
On what they have done
Water spilt like blood
Or hope, or vitriol

Any fellow can be yellow
Who is not at times?
Could courage be a virtue
If fear were not instinct
And mortal dread a crime?
But when that fear feels it appears
As thick in skin and brawn
Posing as if strong
Rights are swiftly sacrificed
And abomination spawned

DEATH IN LIFE

I would phone the Samaritans
Not because I'm about to top myself
But just to tell them I feel like I could
If only I could think of a way
That was pain- and guilt-free
And didn't leave my surviving family members
To pick up, bag up, and burn all the pieces
But I won't be phoning anyone
I wouldn't even know what to say
That I haven't bled onto paper
And stuffed into a burgeoning drawer

I wish I could be with someone
Really with someone
Not a bit player in a power struggle
Shouldering ex-relationship and past life baggage
One eye on the departures board
Wondering if I shouldn't whisk myself off to some
    other
Unknown sorry excuse for somewhere to go
Before she gets the same idea

I wish I could be really alone
Not hiding and hoping I slip by unnoticed
Wishing the world would forget about me
And my debts and embarrassing episodes
Free from the pressure
To compromise, pay my way, say hellos
Eggshells, quicksand and broken glass
And those who can't wait for you to fall on your ass

I wish I had read more books
Soaked up more facts
Sucked up more information
Experienced more experience
I wish I could hold my own in a conversation
Without feeling out of my depth
And yet my references go over the heads
My jokes don't get got
I try to recount what I've been through
With those for whom it doesn't add up
I fumble with gadgets, passwords and apps
Not so easy to pick stuff up
When you can't see the point in getting up

I wish I could stop thinking
About thinking
Analysing everything
To the point where nothing means a thing
I guess the utter, utter pointlessness
Is somehow the point
There's nothing more humbling than
Knowing it only matters if you know it exists
And only for as long as you're around to know
Or remember

I wish I had a faith
I wish I believed in something
I wish I could be an idealist again
I wish there were something
In which I could invest my heart
Not sure if I want to tell all my troubles
Or suffer in silence
Not sure what we have the right to do
Do you?

You can have a life that others envy
But that just makes it empty
At least to me, and who do you want to impress
    anyway?
I try not to be resentful
Bitter
I try not to surrender
A white flag doubles as a shroud
"In the midst of life we are in death"
"We have not begun to live
until we conceive life as a tragedy"
The second quote is ascribed to Yeats
No-one alive knows who said the first first
Epigrams, maxims, aphorisms
Do we know by whom these lines are said?
Do we even care? Does it even matter?
These lines are easier to say when you're dead

DENIAL

Whenever someone says
I'm not a racist
They probably are
Whenever someone says
I'm not a fascist
They probably are
Whenever someone says
I'm not a liar
They probably are
Whenever someone says
I'm not a thief
They probably are

Whenever someone says
I won't tell a soul
They probably will
Whenever someone says
You can trust me
You probably can't
Whenever someone says
I hate you
Don't be too surprised if they don't
Whenever someone says
I love you
Don't be too surprised if they don't

Whenever someone says
I have read and agreed to the terms and conditions
They almost certainly haven't
Whenever someone says
I don't give a fuck
They almost certainly do
Whenever someone says
I know my history
They almost certainly don't
Whenever someone says
Santa won't come if you're not good
He almost certainly will

Whenever someone says
I know it for a fact
You can bet they don't
Whenever someone says
I ain't fucking gay
You can bet they are
Whenever someone says
It's not about money
You can bet it is
Whenever someone says
I'm only doing it for the money
You can bet they aren't

Whenever someone says
I feel great
That was the best sex I've ever had
This tastes wonderful
I really appreciate what you did back there
You look incredible
You're really talented
You make me happy
I can't wait to see you again
Unsolicited
You can bet they're probably telling the truth
And you can bet you'll probably doubt them 'til the
     cows come home
And how many times have you seen cows come
     home?

Whenever you listen to
The voice inside
Be wary of what it says
For anyone able to lie to someone else
Is always better at lying to themselves

THE DEVIL

I first met the Devil
When far too young
To have a clue what it was
It had drawn blood
To exercise dominion
And quash any difference of opinion

It had standards
It demanded
That were hopelessly unattainable
Yet forego
The struggle to reach them
You were strictly unable to
Anything less than your best
Simply would not do
The greatest effort made
Was repaid
By being forbade peace
And an adding to the weight
Of your guilt-filled duty due

I have toiled
Under his watchful gaze
I knew he was beside himself
Waiting for my oh so welcome
Oh so rebuked
Mistake
For which I could take no reasonable blame
But for which I earned thereafter
A knife-twistingly demeaning name

The Devil once told me
Such a lie
It derailed my life
Forcing me onto a one-way street
Guaranteed to collide with defeat
Replete with bunches
Of well-aimed sucker punches

The Devil is known by many a name
And alias
And manifests in many a guise
And uses many a vessel
Mephistopheles
Mastema
Iblis
Erlik
Ahriman
Baphomet
Old Nick
Or sometimes simply Nick
Or Tom or Dick or Harry
Or Marie
Or Miriam
Or Charlie
Or Niaz
Or Matthew Hopkins
Or Coca-Cola
Or gaslighting sadism
Or nonchalant eugenicism
Or a promiser of emancipation
Or razor-toothed character assassination

Oftentimes the Devil calls itself a Christian
Upholder of a nation's laws
The voice of reason, the maker of sense
It scoffs at its own identification
Or a library's immolation
Or mass extermination
Is its self-righteous retaliation

Oh, one other thing
The Devil is profoundly adept
Utterly excels
At persuading itself
It doesn't exist
It twists whatever proof you give it
To ensure its self-denial
And evil presence persists

DIS PLACE

I've been to Czechoslovakia
It no longer exists
I've been to Macedonia
It no longer exists
I've been to Kosovo
Which does/does not exist
Depending on what you recognise
Or who's holding your wrists
In Skopje, I told my hosts
Pristina was where I was next to go
Their faces looked like they'd seen a ghost
Their eyes dropped to tell me they'd rather not know
And I was born in Somerset
But not the same by boundary
As the one you these days get
And Bristol to the north
Was once Avon's county seat
But Avon in '96
Beat a historybound retreat

Many stake a claim
To disputed domains
Many folk hail
From where we wish them well
Or try to put them in their place
Or tell them go to hell
Somaliland
Does not go hand in hand
With Somalia's plan
Or Taiwan
Where a Blue Sky and a White Sun
Glare down upon their errant son
Palestine, surely for sure
Flies the flag for
De facto versus de jure
Is not war
Crime a
More fitting term
For a lot of annexation?
And aren't an awful lot of territorial disputes
Like con- versus transubstantiation?
Do Moldovans speak Moldovan
When in Romania?
And as for Transnistria
It's recognisable only to
The questionable
Abkhazia, Artsakh
And South Ossetia

In Nagorno-Karabakh
The people of Armenia and Azerbaijan
Scream 'Give us our land back!'
In Turkey, Syria, Iraq and Iran
Is the roughly defined Kurdistan
Was there an end to the American Civil War
Did Yankees and Southerners ever settle the score?
And Hungary spills over its borders
And North says South Korea
Can't exist, by order
And if your name happens to be Saudi
You can call a country after your family
And due to half the UK saying no to the EU
And voting for cloud cuckoo cockadoodledoo
Like verbal diarrhoea with muckspreading intent
Some think they're no longer in the continent

Ungaritza bladesmiths
Drift through the mountains like mist
Kalderash bucketmakers
Midway seers, rope climbing fakirs
The Lalleri and Ashkali
The Sinti and Lovari
Those without the wont to own
The self-possessed who want to roam
And The New Colossus
Bid the huddled masses
But did the lamp of Liberty light the way for the
    nation?
There are more than a few who have their
    reservations

Google Maps
Are not rigidly fixed
But relaxed
About what they're displaying
According to what each state dictates
Multibillionaires are every bit
As much slaves to whoever's paying

1.6 billion people
Lack an adequate roof over their head
Countless millions with roofs over their heads
Wish they lived somewhere else instead

The concept of property
Is human vanity
In a world where we all do and don't belong
Where the commonest borrowed term is home
Opulent palatial abodes
Are luxury
Only to those
Who never stop feeling owed
And luxuriate in vulgarity

Countless take their vacations
In imagined nations
Middle Earth, Lilliput, Discworld
Wonderland
Or the Hundred Acre Wood
Or townships that rock
Like Castle Rock

Home is
Where the
Heart is
No wonder too many of us by far
Wonder quite where the hell we are

DOG WHISTLE
WHISTLEBLOWING

88
This ain't bingo
14 words
Know the lingo
The greatest story never told
Do you believe in freedom of code?

Family values
Sovereignty
Our people first
Welfare queens
Old stock
Patriotism
The right to bear arms
'Gainst unAmericanism

Heritage
Honor
Glory
Tradition
God has given me a mission
Hold the Bible high
Othala pin on my black tie

Hard-working
Law and order
Bad hombres
'Cross the border

Global special interest
International banks
Give support to our troops
Show them your thanks

Illegals
Drifters
Scroungers
Layabouts
Forced busing
Inner cities
Benefits
Handouts
Bogus asylum seekers
Taxpayers' expense
Food stamps
Antifa
Nanny state
Coincidence

Confederate flag
My country, my land
Wonder-working power
From my cold dead hand

Semantic
Contextual
Stereotype dependent
At-a-glance innocuous language
But you-know-who knows what you meant

A sly nod to your subset
Ask the rest why they're getting upset
A secret handshake and semantic priming
Implicit attitude and measured timing
A shading of truth and an unchecked lie
And divisiveness is multiplied

Prosody and smokescreened signs
Builds the walls between the lines
Armed with earpiece and offensive charm
You've a litigation-proof call to arms

DUPLICITOUS LIVES MATTER

That word
That R word
It's got to the point
Where we can't help but feel
It's tired from being
Misused and abused
Cheapened and derided
By the one-sided
Short-sighted
Closed-minded
There's many a list
Of terms that exist
That sound hackneyed and clichéd
Let's talk of something else
Unoriginal
The slave trade
There's no longer a golliwog
On the jar of marmalade
And the coffee in your cup
Is Fair Trade
(Also served at Starbucks.
Also sold by Nestlé)

Stupid is
As stupid does
Like prejudiced
Oppressive
And treacherous too
I'm as anti-racist
As someone who says they aren't racist is
As partial in deed as not by declaration
Every bit as much as you

Racists use words
Eat food
Wear clothes
Drive cars
Use gadgets
Etc etc etc etc etc etc etc etc
That are the unconscious heritage
Of cultures they claim to be somehow above

Anti-racists
Eat food
Wear clothes
Study at schools
Work at jobs
Etc etc etc etc etc etc etc etc
Built on the blood and bondage
Of peoples for whom they claim an equal love

We cannot practice what we preach
We can only teach
That what we're all doing is inherently wrong
And try to love our neighbours
Enough for our consciences to favour our flawed
    selves
And somehow, somehow, all try to get along

THE EARTH IS FLAT

What we believe
Might not be
What we think we believe
There are fewer things we do
Better than self-deceive

Play it cool
But fanfare court
Crave acceptance
Fear rejection
Critical thinking
Doesn't get anywhere
Near the applause
Of selective perception

What we say
In the moment
Of a given day
Might only reflect
A passing mood
What seems right
We sometimes mistake
For what at the time feels good

One day Thunberg's a heroine -
A tender failed
A coffee spilt
It's 'Oh god, not her again.'

We parry disfavour
Rattle sabres
In order to express a grudge
Adopt opinion because it clashes
With that of one of whom
We're an unforgiving judge

Someone might say
Something outré
Contrary, against the grain
Approval
Or clash of swords
Thumbs up
Or war of words
Might not matter either way
As long as our attention's gained

Some like to shatter illusions
Because their own conclusions
Failed to spare them
Hurt or confusion
Say that Santa doesn't exist
Because they were put on his naughty list

It's easy to see how
It's easy to believe
In an afterlife
When given to grieve
He loves me?
He loves me not?
Who doesn't like a good ending?
Who's not a fan of a satisfying plot?

The untruthful
Rarely looks the fool
And escapes ridicule
Or gets us into someone's pants
Or our foot in the door of a better chance

Sanctioned falsehoods
A greater good
Intimidation
Cherry-picked confirmation
Context
Threats
Purposes crossed like wires
Can there ever
Really be
Such thing as
An honest liar?

THE _____ IN THE ROOM

We don't say D
Is for Dodo
Do we?
So soon
Will we say
E
Is for Extinct?

Imagine having enough money
To buy the world
And all you want to do is sell it out
Having enough wealth
To have the world's most expensive tastes
But having any sense of it completely go to waste
Is it an unwritten rule
The fatter the numbered
And offshore accounts
The lesser the human values
To which they amount?

Having in excess of 200 billion
And paying 1% tax
It's like being the world's greatest linguist
And refusing to read a word
Having the sharpest vision
And refusing to gaze at a single work of art
A unique ability to show your love
Yet building a solid gold wall 'round your heart

Meanwhile...
In Dzanga Bai
And Garamba
Kruger park
The Okavango Delta
Through Dar es Salaam
And Mombasa
To Vietnam
And China

From Bezos, Branson, Musk...
To Botswanan poachers gouging out tusks
I guess some, no matter what anyone says, don't
    count
I guess some, no matter what anyone says, can't

Life
Is all over in a blink
And it stinks
So we might as well push it to the brink
Send it all down the plughole
Everything but
And including the kitchen sink

E is for Evasion of taxes
E is for Egomaniacal
E is for Ecodevastation
Our all-star billionaires
Have turned their business skills
To colonising the stars
E is for our efforts stolen
Invested in 5-star hotels on Mars

THE EXPLOITED

White exploits black
White exploits white
Black exploits white
Black exploits black
No-one has black skin
Nor white for that matter
We're all exploiting
We're all exploited
However we tailor our patter

The straight exploit the gay
The strong exploit the weak
The smart exploit the dumb
The bold exploit the meek
Husbands exploit wives
Women exploit men
Jerry exploits Tom
Barbie's exploited by Ken

Pornography exploits masturbators
Pornography exploits fornicators
Intimidators exploit and are
Exploited by other intimidators

Employers exploit employees
The first exploit the last
The heart swindles the head
Cults exploit outcasts

Social media cons us
Dopamine tricks our sense
Aggressors are good at exploiting
And labelling it defence

The Exploited exploited their fans
And their label exploited the band
A contrived conflict with Crass
Was how Secret Records forced their hand

People exploit animals
Beasts exploit beasts
We feast on those we've fooled into
Thinking they're at a feast

The haves exploit the have-nots
Then silver tongue themselves
Into buying the idea
Their worth lies in their wealth

Sometimes exploiters trick themselves
Into justifying their exploitation
Sometimes the exploited perceive their fate
As cause for resignation

The world is ruled by bullies
Oligarchs and plutocrats
Power's their addiction
And getting us to do their dirty work for them
Is something for which they certainly have a knack

EXTREMES

What is an extremist?
Is extremism something easily seen?
What exactly does extremism mean?
And what is the alternative?
Lukewarmism?
To be a moderate this or that?
Aren't most of us mild-mannered wannabee
    autocrats?

Can one be an extremist unconsciously?
Who among us aspires to be intolerant?
Or desires to be tolerant?
It's impossible to be anti being anti
It's easy to be pro
What is anti what we thought it meant
Or think it means but wrongly so

Fascism
Tyranny
Oppression
Hard sold
The kind that grips nations
In a stranglehold
Does not announce itself as itself
Nor does it have to do
Its own dirty work
Once the ball gets rolling
Heads follow, as commonplace
As Sunday park strolling

Fanaticism
Is a subconscious expression of doubt
If you believe, you believe
Truth whispers, fear shouts

I like tea
Actually I love it
I adore it
When it comes to tea
I'm an extremist
Down to a T

I prefer
The excitement of novels
The scare factor of horror films
The intensity of drum solos
The heavens above of making love
As extreme as can be
I'm in it to get wobbly at the knees

I'm no adrenaline junkie
Though I am an experience one
So give it all you've got
Look life in the eye
Aim for the G-spot
Give me simple pleasures
That get one to giddying heights
Meted out in dizzying measures

FLYING MONKEYS

I'm a bully but identify as victim
I'm unhygienic but identify as clean
Duplicitous, swear blind I'm honest
I don't even know that I don't know what I mean

Impressionable, tell you I'm nobody's fool
I preach principles, break my own rules
I'm lazy but see me as a grafter
Identify as modest but glory's what I'm after

I'm paranoid but call myself aware
So don't you dare
Don't you dare

I'll insist reason
And compassion
Are akin to treason
And safely out of fashion

Your lips are duct taped
Your hands hogtied
I might be in denial
But my type won't be denied

I am what I say I am
As long as you're afraid
To question's out the question
I am free to be obeyed

Granted approval
I've the backing of the hour
Yours might make more sense
But my voice is louder
My voice is louder
MY VOICE IS LOUDER

FOR THE GRETA GOOD

Are you bored by now
With the end of the world?
We're on the brink of the brink of
The brink of being doomed
Don't you wish it would get a move on?
It's kind of lost its charm
Gone the way of Morrissey
I mean, how soon is soon?

Yesterday's number one splash
Is tomorrow's crashing bore
Seems even saving the lives of one's family
Becomes a victim of its own popularity

Are you going to give up your phone?
Like you gave up on that abstract layer of ozone?
Are you going to give up the car?
Or just bitch the asphalt is molten tar?
Are you going to give up (on the) Amazon?

I hope you recycle
Good advice
Instructions on how to be more nice
That's better than writing derisory verse
That's like recycling despair or worse

All these terms
I'm tired of writing them down
Snowflake, fascist, socialist
Have their meanings hijacked and turned around
Is activist now a dirty word?
Is it inoffensive
To be inactive?
Doesn't it have to strive for something
For anything at all to be attractive?

If the world is our mother
Maybe we want to punish her
After all, did we ask to be born
Only to die?
Thanks for the gift
Of awareness of mortality
Your cycles dance on our graves
Yet saving your ass is morality?

Let's level Aleppo
On our road to Damascus
Outweigh the fish in plastic
And drown in tears of anti-maskers

Now watch as this descends into pathos
Like an ableist into feelings of helplessness...

If you don't believe in climate change
Even if you're right
Even if it's a hoax
Say we follow Greta's advice
What's the worst that could ensue?
Maybe we clean up the planet a little
You know, that place we live?
Maybe plan to keep living
And maybe our future generations too
I request all anti-activists
Put your money where your mouth is
Do not hate
Do not troll
Do not think
And do not do

FOR THE LOVE OF KAREN

Shaking with rage
Is all the rage
Viral feed the new centre stage
The Karens are calling
The callers out of Karens
Karens
I feel a tad sorry for those with the name
Who inopportunely shoulder its shame
First they came for the Shanes and Waynes
The Tracies and Staceys
Then they came for the Sharons
And then…
Yet regardless of mass extermination
There are places where 'Adolf' gets an annual
    celebration

There are no end of idiots among us
Calling Antifa fascists
Calling National Socialists socialists
Saying footballers who get down on their knees
Threaten Christian society
OR preach rights of minorities
On a soapbox of gadgetry
Built on the chattel
Of embattled ethnic majorities
(But I really start to wonder
Can anyone else see the irony?)

Karen/Ken might not be
The miss-ma-stress of diplomacy
But if you ask me
(whispering conspiratorially)
In every woman
There's a little tiny hint of misandry
In every man
The teeniest trace of misogyny
But I'd best think that secretly
Before someone makes a meme out of me

'I know my rights!'
Said nobody who knows their rights ever
But if I ever get to meet the one
Supposedly born in a manger
The first thing I'm going to say to him:
'I WANNA SPEAK TO THE MANAGER!!'

GOING OUT IN STYLE

The greyness of the temple
Might be darkened by
Enlightening meditation
Or dye

The furrows of the brow
Might be ironed out
By iron and magnesium
Or nowt

Crow's feet might be
Stamped out, scared away
By night creams, or night
Seeing off the day

The silver of the beard
Needn't buy one trouble
The riches of experience
Are soon reduced to stubble

The sagging of the flesh
When the knife is out of reach
And the gym a step too far
Can be hidden from the beach

Birthdays come more often now
Than what one know's worth knowing
Things go by faster
As one's haste to get by's slowing

When living feels like dying
Are you in or out your box?
Is that a purring inside you
Or a thing you daren't unlock?

Memories you once treasured
Are ghosts you now see through
What scared you once means nothing
What were angels once are ghouls

Sparks of idealism
Lost fizz and fizzled out
The most gargantuan monsters are
Dwarfed by self-doubt

You're not dead yet!
'Til the cells have had their say
How often do they tell you
Thumbs up, all's A-OK?

Remember when you wished to last
A century or more?
That was a hundred years ago
Yet feels more like a score

The lining of the cloud
The consolation prize
Is they who die alone will be
A hit among blowflies

GOSSIP WELL TOLD

Some will say if you like Picasso
You're a fan of an asshole
Was he as adept at being an artist
As he was a misogynist?
Was Mother Teresa's Christian dream
Damned to end up a Ponzi scheme?
And did Steve Jobs, like Bill Gates
Patent whatever he'd appropriate?
Was Thomas Edison, GE's chief
A technical genius or common thief?
Was Mahatma Gandhi a pacifist
Or a wife-beating racialist?
Did Woodrow Wilson, POTUS 28
Fan the Klan's fires of hate?
And Winston Churchill is quite adored
But likely never by a "blackamoor"
And A G Bell makes the list
Not the phone book but as a eugenicist
Tibet seems a Shangri-la dream
But serfdom and torture propped up its regime
Did Einstein count on counting so well
As on telling his wife to go to hell?
Was Martin Luther's theism
Enhanced by his antisemitism?
Moses is "man of God" to some
But ordered the slaying of unborn sons

Guevara is poster boy of Havana
But was Chief Executioner of La Cabana
And Ford invented the Model T
And inspired the Gestapo, to make history
And Muhammad's revered as a holy prophet
So sweep that underage stuff under the carpet

Our insecurity heroises
Our self-loathing demonises
Our disinclination romanticises
Our doubtfulness idolises
If what we say matters
What we do matters more
What we don't do matters most
And history, for sure
Rarely keeps the score

GRAMMAR
UNTERMENSCH

Two-and-a-half thousand
Authors escaped Germany
Between 1933
And '39
Or, as it was internationally known
(And increasingly statistically unknown)
Nazi Germany, at the time

On May 10th
1933
Unter den Linden
Berlin University
Joseph Goebbels
Gave a speech
To a burning torch procession
Cum ceremony

Thomas Mann
Having said 'Auf Wiedersehen'
Succumbed to crackling flame
Heinrich Mann
Having uttered 'Lebewohl'
Turned to ashes too
Remarque
Having bid 'Mach's gut'
Took to the air as soot
Zola
Having been accused
Went the way of six million Jews
Einstein
Due to physical equation
Was toasted 'midst the conflagration
London
It so transpired
Was used to help to build a fire
Wells
Burned and curled
In the second War of the World
Sinclair
Like the Helicon
Was tried by acts of arson

4,000 titles were seized
25,000 volumes
Fed the pyre
And soon there followed more
A total of thirty-four

Marx
Freud
Hesse
Kafka
Grosz
Bauhaus
Hašek
Luxemburg
Hugo
Fitzgerald
Hemingway
Keller
Conrad
Huxley
Lawrence
Joyce
Wilde
Dostoyevsky
Nabokov
Brecht
Among the countless names
Whose work they sought to erase

Thankfully
At the cost of an estimated 80 million lives
The Third Reich was defeated
Freedom of speech among those who survived
Enabling us
Whenever anyone points out a mistake in our
    spelling
Or punctuation
Or conjugation
To idly
Dismissively
Nonchalantly
Or bloody-mindedly
Refer to them
With a lower case 'n'
As a "grammar nazi"

THE HARM PRINCIPLE

You're entitled to your view
It'll be there anyway
No-one needs permission,
Approval or scorn
So don't bother reminding anyone of the above
It's like asserting your birthright
To have been born

You can think what you like
About immigration
Race relations
Sexual orientations
The environment
The government
Cement
You will do anyway

You can concern yourself
With your neighbour's style of hair
Your only-ever-seen-by-your-boyfriend underwear
Your status update
If they were joking or serious, if they're gay or
    straight
Someone you believe has had a luckier break than
    you
Or whether bora bora or fresh cut pine would make
    the best scent for the loo

It's easier to have an opinion
Than explain reasons for it
At every moment we're preaching to a choir
At every moment we're told we're full of shit

There's free speech
And hate speech
Duplicity
And practice what you preach
Irony
Comedy
Context
And appropriacy
Crossed wires
The politically correct
Reappropriation
The truth elect
Censorship
Linguistic drift
The between the lines
And semantic shift

Whatever the purported conviction
Whatever the desired intention
Imparting wisdom or playing the fool
It's better to be cruel to be kind
Than to be the kind that's cruel to be cruel

'They shoulda just told the jumper "Jump!",'
Said the barstool toxic masculinist
'The whole lot of 'em should be sterilised,'
Said the idle chatter eugenicist
'Fine. Whatever,'
Said the staffroom passive-aggressivist
'You don't like it, go back where you came from,'
Said the jerkwater apologist
'You're a total loser,'
Said the dime store supremacist
'Chillin' with a fit bitch,'
Said the postmodern sexist
'I respect...'
'I admire...'
'I enjoy...'
'I love...'
Which of these, if not voiced
Was being felt by the above?

I CAN'T STAND REFUGEES

Were you born in your backyard?
Were your parents born in your backyard?
Were their parents born in your backyard?
Were your entire ancestry born in your backyard?
Did you ever move
From one country to another?
From one town to another?
From a village to a town?
Or city?
Did you ever dream
Of moving somewhere better?
Of course you did
Of course you did

So would you remain in your home
If your home were being shot at?
If your town were being bombed?
If you were struggling to find work?
Or had none at all?
If you were struggling to support your family?
If you wanted to save your children's lives?
If you wanted them to have a fair chance?
If you wanted them to be happy and well?
If you were a woman
And were denied basic human rights
Denied the chance to show your face
Denied a voice
Denied the right to freedom of movement
If you were gay
In a nation of homophobia
Where non-heterosexuality was a capital offence
Or even just heavily stigmatised
If the crops had failed
If drought had claimed the land
If a natural disaster
Had destroyed entire towns
If you faced racism on a daily basis
If you were bullied
If you were persecuted
To the degree where it eroded your confidence
And put you in danger
And ravaged your mental health
If the country you lived in went to war

For reasons unexplained

And inexplicable

To satisfy the needs of men's egos and men's
business

At no benefit to you whatever the result

Would you stand and take it

Roll over and be raped by it

And submit your children to it

If you thought you had a chance

However slim

Based on information and propaganda

You had no means of verifying one way or the other

But felt it was your best chance

Maybe the only chance

You would ever get

Would you take it?

It would take more unimaginable bravery

That those sipping their Proseccos

Supping their cappuccinos

Guzzling their beers and using slurs like 'queers'

On their laptops and iPhones

Blithely sharing right-wing memes

Have likely ever shown

On a single day

Of their resentful

Unsatisfied

Lives

Would you take it?

Would you take it
At the risk of being called lazy
By the believers in and peddlers of easy answers?
Would you take it
At the risk of being called bogus
By those who accept discrimination at face value?
Would you take it
At the risk of attracting racism
From those ignorant enough to believe in the
   scientifically-denounced concept of race?
Would you take it
At the risk of being called scroungers
By those whose labour is ripped off unchallenged by
   tax-dodging corporations?
Would you take it
At the risk of being called terrorists
By those who would nonchalantly send you back to
   a warzone?
Would you take it
At the risk of being called parasites
By those mean and mealy-mouthed enough they
   would not give your children a chance?
Would you take it
At the risk of being called a threat to a sovereignty
By those who believe their nation's constitution is to
   reject compassion?

Would you take it

At the risk of being called an economic immigrant

By those who would not hesitate to call anyone not
actively trying to better their circumstances a
loser?

Or would you be like all those who would reject
refugees

And immigrants

At face value

Because it's always at face value, whatever they say

And stand in the path of bullets

And stand under the dropping of bombs

And stay and starve in the grip of famine

And drought

And deny themselves the chance to escape abuses of
human rights

As a woman

As a man

As a child

And let themselves

Be beaten

Tortured

Raped

Abused

And let their children be beaten

And let their children be tortured

And let their children be raped

And let their children be abused

Because what's important is
If a few people who are potentially dangerous
Or potentially lazy
Or potentially might steal the job you hate
Or would never yourself do
Or potentially might not 'respect your culture'
That you yourself do not understand and know
    profoundly little about
Are denied refugee status
Justice has been served

Everyone is a refugee or immigrant
Or was born of refugees or immigrants
Or has a lineage of refugees or immigrants
There isn't a single exception in the world
I can't stand immigrants
Who say they hate immigrants
I can't stand the gay
Who say they hate the gay
I can't stand idiots
Who say they can't stand idiots
And to really hate refugees
You really have to hate yourself

JUDGING THOSE WHO JUDGE

'Don't be judgmental'
She told me
I guess it was an order
I'm not sure what triggered it though
I don't remember voicing my opinions
On her mother
Who was busy verbally sending gypsies to death
   camps
On her daughter
Who had no time for a thank you or please
Not even her son
Whom she never went a day
Without cursing
Nor was my opinion solicited
On anything worth having an opinion on
In my opinion
But I kept that to myself

I told her her bottom did not look fat and round
Which was a half-truth
Although personally I find larger ones sexier
But who cared about my opinion anyway?
'No, your legs do not look fatter than her legs.'
That was another half-truth
Or half-lie
For a nanosecond's sneak peek
Was hardly time to check out both

'You think you're better than others.'
'You think you're superior.'
I'm not sure what triggered that either
Certainly had I believed everything she told me
    about myself
A subject she appeared quite the expert on
And was privy to information that was unbeknown
    to me
My confidence would have been so shattered
It might almost have been as low
As her own

And although she didn't appear to have it for
    anything worth celebrating
She never lacked passion
When it came to putdowns, criticisms
And character assassination
Or should that be
Wannabee annihilation?

107

The longer we knew each other
The more reticent I became
Yet still she told me about myself
She said I was a liar
(Well, there was the white one about the bum)
A thief
Selfish
Nasty
And swear words, an assortment of
However
What seemed to be worse
Than the idea I might have been a thief or liar etc.
Was the idea I was low class
Apparently
And whatever that might mean exactly
(And whether or not it was at loggerheads with what
    she had earlier said)
Not of the pedigree of the various aforementioned
    people
I had not expressed my opinion on openly
That was a favourite, shall we say, quibble of hers
Choosing language to make her point
Hardly reminiscent of *corps d'elite*
While I buried myself in a used book
And she in resentment
She was not living in a gold-paved street

I know what humble means
I know what down feels like
I even know what adversity is
Why shouldn't I?
I think the words 'I love you' are as beautiful as they
    are fragile
I'm not interested in whether or not
Someone has a hole in their sock
In addition to the one they put their foot into
I am interested in what someone is reading
Or if they read at all
Why shouldn't I be?
I often refer to the IMDb
When selecting a film to watch
I like to read Amazon reviews of books
I believe in a pat on the back
A thumbs up
A well done
When impressed by someone's achievements
Why shouldn't I?
Does this make me judgmental?
Of course it does
As are we all

Judging is something we do
As a survival mechanism
And if we could switch it off
We'd have to switch off thinking

I don't care what colour someone is
What nationality someone is
What sex someone is
I don't have to go to bed with them
How much money they have
Unless it's a crooked fortune
What class they were born into
What is class anyway?
I do care if they tell me not to be judgmental
I judge them as someone somewhat developmental
Why shouldn't I?

I think the more someone accuses others of lying
The more likely they lie themselves
The less they trust others
The less we can trust them
Or they trust themselves
And the more outspokenly against judging they are
The more judging they are

Don't confuse judging
With prejudice
Judging is inescapable
Prejudice inexcusable
In my
Unsolicited
Opinion
Which you're welcome
And guaranteed
To judge

KARMA GETS ITS PAYBACK

If karma were a computer program
We'd likely call the bugbusters in
If it happened to be a Catholic
The priest would hear of a fair few sins
In the case it were a close one
We'd book them a visit to the doc's
In the event it were a vehicle
We'd change the oil, sparks and shocks

Who doesn't ask themselves
How did that guy get that job?
Why is that angel sat in jail?
Who made that one a cop?
Why are all my picnics planned
On days the rain won't stop?
Are we wearing a frown to figure it out
Or simply smelling a crock?

Don't we all have a moral compass?
All have a sense of right and wrong?
All have a gut feeling of guidance?
Is it just the will will not stay strong?
Is fate's fickle finger sick?
Is god the eternal jester?
If virtue is its own reward
Are the virtuous just self-interested investors?
Some say if you sow a thought
So you shall reap a deed
That when that deed is done
It's a habit you will seed
A habit that's adopted
Is character that's born
And it's our character decides
Whatever destiny we've won

Karma's really not easy to define
And definitions vary and are often contrary
For some it's reward, punishment, or revenge
And if it really is a thing, is it something we can
   comprehend?
The Sanskrit into English does not smoothly translate
It's more action, deed and work than it is fate
We can call it good or bad, we can say it's a bitch
Is it kind of being rich while kind of not being rich?

We are what we are
We are not what we have
Sepsis can buy one sympathy
A Corvette C8 can crash
As violence begets violence
And greed can't get enough
Is it our sins we're punished for
Or our sins themselves that punish us?

'Sangha', to me, is goodwill to all
'Cetana', I believe, being focused on goals
'Dukkha' helps us to come to terms with pain
Whether we're the pits or whether we're it
Shit happens time and again

Apparently Gautama
Told of three poisons
We turn into their opposites
As is life's lesson
Greed to generosity
Aggression to compassion
Ignorance to making sense
That is, is it not, karma in action?

ME TOO

All of us have and have been abused
All of us have and have been used
All of us have and have been mistreated
All of us have and have been cheated

None of us have the right to lie
While playing a role as fake as glass eyes
None of us have the right to hurt
While funding those for whom we're dirt
None of us have the right to steal
While robbing ourselves of how we feel
None of us have the right to be unfair
While shielding those who grab our share

Some of us are the victims of rape
Some of us think of death as escape
Some of us are the victims of violence
Some of us are the victims of silence

Each of us has a duty to care
While smarting as the nerve ends tear
Each of us has a duty to aid
While fearing how good deeds are repaid
Each of us has a duty to try
While waving dream after dream goodbye
Each of us has a duty to mend
While raging against the inevitable end

Many of us are in denial
Many of us didn't get a fair trial
Many feel bad they were taken to task
Many feel mad they were never asked

Most of us wish we could start again
While grasping nothing could be more vain
Most of us wish for a world more just
While praying for amends on turning to dust
Most of us wonder what's going on
While trying to figure where the hell we belong
Most aren't sure what we're trying to achieve
While believing whatever we want to believe

THE MOST BESTIAL OF BEASTS

From old school fascism
To neo-Nazism
From self-loathing
To outright sadism
We instinctively feel that cruelty is wrong
So look for an excuse to indulge in it
And a scapegoat to pin it upon

When he choked the life
Out of George Floyd
Was Derek Chauvin's duty
To protect and to serve?
An act no remotely
Sensitive soul
Can dwell upon without losing their nerve
It wasn't enough to take his life
He had to take his hope
And dignity
Force him into a pre-death abyss
And spit in the face of humanity

Was Mengele interested
In the results
Of medical research
Wreaking murder after injury after insult after
    assault?
If you get the green light from pharma giants
If you're sponsored by a scientific elite
Does this cushion the guilt
Of the corpses at your feet?
Does it give mass infanticide
The licence and cover it needs to hide?

When someone says
'I believe in white supremacy.
You're refusing me the right to freedom of speech.'
Aren't they the types
For whom a difference of opinion
Costs those who disagree the price of their teeth?

Do the abused
Always end up as abusers
Or are those who commit
The most inexcusable acts
The biggest self-excusers?

In the UVF
And the IRA
The LAPD
And the NRA
And every other initialism
That try to hold sway
There are those whose fight for justice
Is overpowered by their desire
To wade into the fray

From Josef Stalin
To a terrace hooligan
Kicking the other team's supporter's head in
From Vlad the Impaler
To a troll who tells an uninviting stranger
How he'd love to nail her
From Saddam Hussein
To those who'd film your fatal accident
Then upload your pain
From Idi Amin
To the stag party lairy
Giving a passerby one on the chin
From Himmler's final solution
To those who bathe in the blood
Of bloody revolution
Matthew Hopkins, Leopold, Khan and Pol Pot
Robspierre and anyone
Who'd love to chop your head off
For being what they're not

The cruel at heart
Will invariably say
They're just telling it like it is
I say, in a cruel world
The harbouring of a soft heart
Is the only integrity that exists

NOMOPHOBIA

When it comes to Muslims
Don't get me started
On those among them who walk among us
Texting

I don't need to see gay couples
Together in public
Publicly displaying
How they are so immersed in their phones, they
    seem to have forgotten each other exists
It disgusts me

The other day I saw a homeless man
He didn't have a phone
Not even a tablet
He was talking to himself
And passersby
Why can't more of us be like him?
I thought to myself
I might even have said it out loud

A person might say
The Roman Catholic church
And nationalism
When combined
Produce a chemical reaction
Called fascism
Down a phone glued to their ear
Traversing the concourse of a busy shopping centre
Not really looking where they are going and getting
    in people's way
I might personally find that offensive

You can call me a Remoaner
If you think it's worth complaining about
Or a snowflake
A libtard
A loser
A feminist
A feminazi even
Is that possible?
But don't, for pity's sake, yell these things at me
    down the phone
One hand on the wheel
Swerving to avoid oncoming vehicles
People might get hurt

And if you're black
And fail to see your child's precariously close to the
     roadside
Because you're glued to your iPhone's display
I'll be disappointed in you
Plus a nearing driver
Might just be a Tory voter
With a more expensive phone than yours
Gripped in his dirty paw

PAUSING ON THE BANKS OF THE RUBICON

The road has many forks
Maybe as many as the cutlery drawer
Of the Chinese army's catering corps

Bravery or cowardice
Effort or laziness
Loins or loyalty
Tradition or novelty
Spend or save
Head or heart
Short- or long-term
A rescue package or a fresh start

Inebriation or sobriety
If I choose the latter, my environment needs to be
    alcohol-free
That's really not not drinking successfully

What about whataboutism?
Is the grand scheme of things a vast array of
    schisms?
I wish I'd (never) done, If only I had (not)
The way you thought it might have gone
You really think that's what you'd've got?

How often do your own plans
Meet with their own demands?
It's infectious when someone laughs out loud
But that's rarely the case if it's coming from the
    clouds

Coffee or tea?
Relatively easy
Lies, loans, infidelities
Simple as to say yes please
A cinch to find yourself on your knees

Wouldn't it be cool to have a clone
Or an army of clones?
Not just be you and you alone?
You could have married both them and them
Could have stayed where you were and gone there
    back when
Followed your dream as well as that of theirs
About whatever, you could both have and have not
    cared

But all those inner conflicts, the wars within your
    thoughts
Giving, taking blame; all you owe and all you ought
Clones might form alliances or splinter cells
Help or fight each other. And who and how to tell?

The days are too short
And too numbered
With too many decisions
Hard decisions
And even when sure what's, for the sake of, right
Will you have what it takes
When you come to face that fight?

PERFECT RIGHT

Every Moslem
Each and every one
Which totalled well over a billion
Was eradicated
To put it gently
Every copy of the Qur'an destroyed
Every mosque demolished
All trace of Mohammed's legacy
Liquidated
Islam was no more
As if it had never existed
It was like the Crusades
But even better

Our Leader
(For those of us who remained)
Was asked if he was pleased
Now that his strict orders
Had been hastily yet meticulously carried out.
'Not yet!' he emphatically intoned.
'We have only just started.
We must claim our rightful place.
The most absolutely pure among us are to be
    venerated above all.'

Every Jew
Was snuffed out
Systematically
Efficiently
Synagogues razed
Israel levelled
The Torah history
(But removed from history)
It was like Birkenau
But more glorious still

'Has everything been accomplished to one's
    satisfaction, Our Leader?'
Asked the Deputy Commander of the Realm
A trifle nervously.
'Are you insane?' barked Our Leader
'This is no time to be glib, you fool.'

Everyone black
Asian
Latino
Every non-Caucasian
Was obliterated
To put it mildly
That was an awful lot of people
An awful lot of awful people
Leaving a former minority
The sole human inhabitants of Earth

Our Leader was restless
Those close to him shared the opinion he seemed
    even less at ease
Than ever before

Every homosexual
Lesbian
Bisexual
Trans- this and that
L and G and B and T
And Q
Was annihilated
To put it euphemistically
Only heterosexuals survived the
Cleansing
Any aberration
Became thereafter
A capital offence
To be dealt with
Without delay

Our Leader paced and paced
Up and down
Frowning

Every communist
Socialist
Trade unionist
Liberal
Anyone to the left
Of the ill-defined centre
Was removed from the equation

'You seem troubled, Our Leader.'
'Of course I'm troubled!
Don't tell me you have failed to notice
This poison in our midst??'

Any woman
Thinking themselves equal
In rights and importance
To their masculine superiors
Was educated as to their errors
In a lesson they would remember
The rest of their lives
All the three long hours of it

Our Leader let it be known
Something was weighing him down

Pagans, Wiccans
Polytheists
Atheists
Heathens
And their myriad heresies
All those sinful enough
To reject that they were a sinner
Before the eyes of God
Were fittingly crucified

Idiots
Those too dopey to manage simple arithmetic
Or read or write
Being of no good use to anyone
Were pushed off the edge of a tall cliff
Why waste bullets?
Those with two left hands too
For good measure

The ginger-haired
And freckle-faced
Being far from fanciable
And odd-smelling
Were put out of their misery
And that they caused others

The short
The ungainly
The below-average-looking
Went the way
Of the physically
And mentally
Ill and disabled
South of the ground

Our Leader sat, slumped
His eyes downcast.
The Deputy Commander was worried.
'The people from the neighbouring village,' his
    superior divulged.
'I've been hearing rumours…
We cannot afford to take any chances.'

Soon, the world's population was down to just
    double figures
All of them the chosen ones
The supermen
With their God-given right
The Deputy visited upon Our Leader
'We have had discussions,' he declared
'In my absence??' demanded Our Leader
'In your absence, sir.
We have come to the conclusion
I am now the fittest
Healthiest
Most allegiant
There is.
Your position
By all rights
Should be handed over to me.'
'What is this sacrilege??'
'Sir, you, as the fellow chosen and I have agreed
Are subordinate only to me.
My loyalty cannot be questioned.
We will simply exchange our places.
You shall become my rightful Deputy.
"The most absolutely pure among us are to be
    venerated above all.".'

Our Leader thought
For lingering seconds.
'Yes,' he agreed.
'How right you are.'
He pulled his gun from its holster
And shot his Deputy dead.
'How right you are.'

132

POOR YOU

You work hard
At telling us you work hard
Or at least that there are people who do
You pay taxes
Just like everyone
Who has ever bought a pot noodle
You moan about dole scroungers
That minorities have the majority say
About refugees having state-gifted houses
And immigration's why you're underpaid

It must be hard not being a gypsy
It must be a bitch not being unemployed
Tough not to have to leave the country you were
    born in
It's easy to see why you're annoyed
If only you too were a Jew
If you only had the luck of the Irish and black
A tragedy you have a roof over your head
How despairing not to lack what you cannot say you
    lack

They're making it possible for gay couples
To have marital rights like heterosexuals
And then they're allowing them to adopt
Me, my spouse and my children are shocked

As part of psychosocial rehabilitation
Children get sent on tax-funded vacations
My parents never took me on a holiday
Yet kids' home residents have dream getaways

Our nation sends money as foreign aid
Instead of helping me to get laid
We have our own share of beggars galore
I see as I walk past them on my way to the store

We shouldn't let people into this country
From war zones, in the interests of safety
As the EDL, BNP and Britain First advise
We can't guarantee they're the nicest of guys

I must be missing something
The less I have
The more I feel
For those who have less than me
A little less misery in someone's world
Is a world with a little less misery
Is it unfairness that makes you go spare
Or are you binging on twinges of envy?
Hate a freeloader gratuitously
While a hundredth are 99% tax-free

I once saw a comment that read
That striking firefighters
Spend most of their workday
Sitting around waiting for a blaze
Taking it easy
Chilling out for a wage
An easy job, they said
And, all things considered,
Not so badly paid.
Even if that were true,
I thought to myself,
It must be a pity
There are not more fires
Not more lives in danger
That a firefighter doesn't face more risks
That not more buildings go up in flames
To justify whatever ends up in their pockets
Luckily I'm not a firefighter
I think I'd feel ashamed

PSYCHIC NUMBING

Is it just me
Or do folk in general have more difficulty
Dealing with that which dealt ill fame
To Soham
Than what brought the same
To the WTC
Which in turn dwarfed
Kosovo
Paradoxically diminishing
Rwanda in tow?

I fill up my head
With dialectical materialism
Go to bed with
Absurdities of existentialism
I try to split the atom
Of metaphysics
Pick the deadlock of my dread
'Midst multiple memorised lyrics
Ignoring niggling physical ails
The dearth of pension for the end of my tale
My tatterdemalion hand-me-downs
And losing the plot 'fore I'm lost underground

How far is it to...?
It's a long way
From one end o' village t' other
Not quite so much bother
To venture a couple of counties, brother
A mere six hours on the Interstate
Now 'we've' been to Mars
Infinitely harder, I hear
Than crashing the pearly gates

28,000 in the Boer camps
(I had to consult Google for the figure)
The beehive-from-hell barneted Hindley
Is a boogeywoman that's somehow bigger
How many lost in the Trail of Tears?
Yet the Son of Sam summed up the States' fears
Asiatic Vespers are reduced to whispers
And FGM victims our forgotten sisters

Johns Hopkins provides the list
Of all who've succumbed
All who desist
Funny how all those zeroes
Start to look like nothing

Through one end of the binoculars
The world appears to be smaller
Reversed, distant figures
Look multiple times taller
We choose how we want to build things up
Or how we play them down
Like the qualities within ourselves
The important
Trivial
Tragic
Comedic
It depends what it is we want to be found

QUICKSILVER PROMISES

Mary washed her hands
A hundred plus times a day
Before it became epidemic
For the rest of us to meet her quarterway
Terrified of contamination
She scrubbed and scrubbed but fear remained
'Til her coarse reddened fissured palms
Got infected as reward for her pains

Will had to have a certain woman as his own
A woman he had dated who had then underrated
How perfect things could be
If she chose him, and him alone
Her attention had been distracted
She had interacted
With someone who could never love her as much
With such
Devotion, adulation, adoration
Needing to get the message across
Will let her know
Were there any further signs
She might entertain the delusion
This other...loser might be her beau
He would kill him
Then her, then himself
In that order
If that did not convince her…
Through force of Will
With the zeal and insistence and determination
Of Bokassa I on his coronation
He made her abide to be his bride
Now even in hot weather, she keeps her body
    covered
Will never looks relaxed
Never looks happy
She would never ever dare cheat on him
But he wears a look of someone who's been cheated
    inside

Earl was proud
With a capital P
Fred Perry polo on his back
No Goodyears on his SUV
Voice spoke of free speech stolen
Arms of NRA
His chest of 6MWE
His hands of OK
But Earl's great grandpappy
With whom he shared DNA
Had changed his name from Liebermann
When fleeing Deutschland
For the good ol' USA

Vlad managed
Like a boss
To obtain an outlandish gain
From an undetected loss
To a state budget
Skimming
Scamming
With precision cunning
A Svengali
A Machiavelli
With the kind of stony glare
That turned critics and challengers to jelly
Moonrock-made Meteoris on his wrist
Those who chose
To try to expose him
Ceased to exist
Proxies, shells, shadows and banks
No-one outranks
The embezzlement-made self-styled tsar
(His dog's kennel's rumoured to have a wraparound
    bar)
Someday soon he's going to glean
Enough of a giddying sum
To outlaw opposition, censor any blog
Buy up all the forests and turn them into logs
To feed the growing yet underwhelming fires
Of his unappeasably ravening desires

Whatever it is we want
Or might want
Or think we want
Are told we want
If we only have an ear
For reasons
Not to listen to reason
If our goals neglect respect or are numb to sense
If the rewards we crave
Turn others into slaves
If we bankrupt our conscience
And force others to foot the expense
We might well learn after the fact
Mutations of fate don't give tuppence
For the Trades Description Act

Like Mr and Mrs White
The world has quite enough fools
Too weak, too myopic to resist the draw
Of a mummified monkey's paw

ROCKET SCIENCE

We've been to the moon
And back, I guess
Six times, nothing more, nothing less
Well, OK, not you, exactly
And most certainly not me
You know how difficult it is for men
To aim it at the porcelain
Let alone guide
A tin can through space
However, we say man on the moon
Were women invited?
I'm not sure why they would want to go
It wouldn't surprise me in the slightest
If they had something better to do
(Like, once their husband has finished in there
Astronaut or not
Clean the loo)
Anyway
I like to say
Al-leg-ed-ly went to the moon
It really makes no odds to me whether they did or
    not
I just get a kick
At seeing how quickly armchair scientists
Leap out of their seat
In a fit of pique

One of the most heartbreaking things
To which I've ever borne witness
Was a heavily pregnant woman
Sifting through the contents
Of public trash cans
Presumably in search of something to eat
I did not stop to ask her
Who ever does?
It's not the kind of thing that
Once viewed
Can ever be unseen
I did not try to find out
Whatever put someone in her condition
(Or in any, for that matter)
In such circumstances
Who ever would?
Plus I was in a hurry
Who ever isn't?

I know it's no fun to hear about it
Imagine how it was to see it
Imagine how it must be to be it

The James Webb Space Telescope
Is something that will allow
People cleverer than you or me
To look at light
From outer space
In ways that excites them
The estimated cost
Is 8.8 billion dollars
I'm not sure where people get
The kind of funding
For that calibre of tin can
But am pretty certain
They didn't happen upon it
Whilst sifting through the contents
Of a trash can

I wonder if
If it were possible to build a tower
Of pennies
To the total of 8.8 billion dollars
It would reach as high
As to leave the Earth's atmosphere

Taking one extreme
And then another
And juxtaposing them
Putting contrasts together
That really have nothing to do with each other
In order to make
Some kind of vague dramatic point
Knowing you'll be outargued
By those you've triggered
Who can quote names and dates
And know their facts and figures
Is a pretty cheap shot
But when your salary
And IQ
Are as modest as mine
That's the best shot you've got

People like me
Are ignorant
Unintelligent
Unappreciative
Taking everything for granted
Or are too busy moaning
To contribute much at all
There are countless people
Smart people
Of upstanding character
Enough to stretch to Cape Canaveral and back
Who know what they're talking about
Who would give the thumbs up
To the James Webb whatsamacallit
And I bet none of those
Would be daft enough
To allow themselves
To find themselves
Homeless, hungry and pregnant
Or short enough of pennies
That they have to sift through trash

RUSSIAN GOSSIP

Whether your partner
Your mother
Your child
Greta Thunberg
The meek and mild

A monogamous lover
Zuzana Čaputová
A holy dog
Your pet god

Jeremy Corbyn
The diseased
The deceased
Angela Merkel
Amnesty International
The WHO
Or Greenpeace

There will be a skeleton there
Somewhere
Amidst the cobwebs and dust
Of all the closeted clutter and must

Who would disbelieve it's there?
Everyone had their moment of abandon
Their cheat sheets
Their lack of modesty
Their taking credit they didn't deserve
Their soiled underwear

Whether Saddam Hussein
Kim Il-sung
A school bully
Or Eichmann

A toreador
Hindley
John Wayne Gacy
Or Mussolini

Whoever shopped Anne Frank
Raiffeisenbank
A violent, abusive spouse
Or Václav Klaus

Somewhere
If you look hard enough
If you are determined
Enough
There will be something commendable there
I'm not saying you should
But be they parents
Lawyers
The Odal runed
Or Stockholm Syndromed
There are those who would

It's not just who's shot down in flames
It's also who's doing the shooting
It's not just hallowed be thy name
But who's doing the trumpet tooting
What's the agenda and intention?
What's the source and why the mention?
Do they seek to unearth truth
Or do they make do without proof?
Is it self-loathing
In woolly-argumented clothing?
Jealousy? Incisiveness?
Consistency? Divisiveness?
Whoever's raised or razed
Whatever's been appraised
Be sceptical of that that's shared
That's been defensively declared

SARTRE'S NAUSEA

Initially, existential crisis
Feels like a passing black hole for happiness
For you've plenty more years to exist
Yet it persists, and persists, and persists

What used to hit the spot was music
What used to be the answer was books
Dissent, and defending the environment
But the mere Death of God was all it took

Food can be good
But you're choked by the unpalatable
Films can be cool
The big pic insurmountable
Travel might rock
Still you're stuck somewhere terrible
Sex can be hot
But you burn with the unbearable
Kids need feeding
But the vacuum is voracious
Money needs earning
The voices whisper 'Sisyphus'
You laugh like a fool
For it's so gravely serious
You're molecules but
Insignificance is onerous

You think therefore you're a nihilist
In the theatre of the absurdest
A solitude-craving soliloquist
Ailed by unto death sickness

You used to scratch out hurt with pencil
Used to blot out pain with pen
Mist would drift with mysticism
'Til the dark night of the neverend

If there is no meaning
Why is it one we crave?
If we cannot be saved
Why the yearning to be saved?
How do we, disillusioned, fill the void
With our victories nulled
By the dream having been destroyed?

With everything rendered ridiculous
Everything pointing to pointlessness
There's no real escape
Bar fleeting retreats
From the phenomenologically bleak

Hooked on religion, devoted to addiction
Placated by romance, or sutured by art
To be mentally sound, a fractured mind is needed
For who can love another without a broken heart?

THEM OR US

That beggar covered up with litter-bulging bags
Bidding sleep in a skip like a soiled rag
The bearer of contusions from a beating from their
    spouse
Poverty arrested whilst ashamed to leave their house
Boat-crammed hundreds on an unforgiving sea
Fleeing famine, then starved strategically
Stateless internees barred hygiene for weeks
Orphans accompanied by strangers' shrieks
Those raped and mutilated 'midst the spoils of war
The traffickers' prisoner dismissed as some pimp's
    whore
The uninsured diseased who can't afford their meds
Sleep-deprived textile slaves hanging by a thread
The toxins-encrusted in undocumented mines
The debt-enslaved swindled by small print between
    lines
Prescription addicts with mood swings on the slide
Exterminated vermin in acts of genocide

Might just as well
Could just as easily
Be you

You don't think it could ever end up that way?
How many do you think once thought
They were exempt from suchlike too?

And if you refuse to see it that way...

The banker foreclosing on an ailing retiree
Installers of anti-homeless spikes on streets
Those who slay a sibling to be member of a gang
The Mount Paektu Bloodline ordering bloodshed
    from Pyongyang
Lockheed Martin's gun runners greased with Saudi
    oil
The dowry demanding dousing brides with vitriol
The Aryan Brotherhood with "blood in, blood out"
    pledge
The deep web red room with its livestreamed razor's
    edge
Cyberstalkers denigrating strangers at their whim
Those for whom war trophies are hacked off
    children's limbs
Pharma giants upping price a thousandfold and
    more
Arsonists burning ancient forests to their floor
The 1% investing in tax avoidance schemes
Parents taking pleasure in destroying children's
    dreams
Zero hour contractors demeaning harried staff
Schadenfreude's seething grin and noxious barren
    laugh

Might just as well
Could just as easily
Be you

TO HELL WITH YOU TOO

After queuing
And queuing
For ever
And an hour
No chair to spare
Finally
Her turn came
To be talked to
Like an errant dog
Owned by errant owners
No-one, it seemed, had time
For pleasantries
Or pleasantness
Or courtesy
Or smiles
And when she dared to wear one
Upon her pensive face
She was looked upon as she were a paedophile

He started putting his groceries on the belt
The cashier started
Putting her wrath on display
'The light's red! Can't you see??'
He could, quite clearly
'It's green. Actually.'
But her mood was as black
As a colourless life
'This checkout. Is closed!' she shrieked
Ordering him to shut his beak

'Excuse me,' I said to the driver
'Does this bus go to-'
'The destination's on the front display!'
He barked before I could go any further
'But there's nothing written on the front display,' I
    told him
He checked to find I was right
Wordlessly and angrily grunted
When nothing more was forthcoming
I repeated my original question
This time managing its completion
'Yes!' he spat, as if a curse
Giving me a looking over
As if wanting to run me over
Or worse

Are not the thorns in your side
When you're prickly multiplied?
Is your self-preservation
Really pre-emptive strikes?
Do the breaths you take have
The whiff of Zyklon B?
Do the words you leave hanging
Resonate like 'kike'?

The golden rule
Easy as pie to apply
A piece of cake to break

Pity those whose manner
Tells strangers to go to hell
For who does so who does not feel
Their place is there as well?

2020 VISION
(IN HINDSIGHT)

I've heard it said that 50 is the most important
   birthday
Mine, which happened six months before
The year 2020 or, to some, 1984
Was largely off the radar
I can honestly say
For me, that was kind of OK

I'm an ardent fan of dystopian tales
I'm certain every second seasoned reader
Harbours half an entertained hope
The end of the world, when all go to hell
Is an event they will witness firsthand
If not something they will live to tell

The year was ushered in on a red carpet
Of wildfires carbonising
The largest land mass in Oceania
Koala, kangaroo, and cockatoo
Toxins in the lungs of the world at large
Species on the brink of survival
Tears can't extinguish a conflagration
Ecodevastation marked the year's mere arrival

Neil Peart
Died
How…? Hey…? What…? But…?
He was just one of millions
But he was one in millions

Whispers drifted in from the Far East
At the outset, a mere moment's ripple
Disturbing the peace
Or general unease
Another epidemic; we were afraid we'd die from
    yawning
Heard it all before. Yes, yes, how boring

Suddenly, the ignorant masses
Distracted by kittens, antipathy and flashed asses
Became an army of epidemiologists
Virologists, conspiracists, and omniscientists who
    got the gist
We've been had
By China
Or by the white coated in labs
But we need the white coated
Some more than others
The monotopical became anything but a drag

George Floyd
Was to become a household name
Of posthumous ill-fated fame
As was Derek Chauvin
To become a new boogeyman
An act of unimaginable
Protracted
Suffering
Cruelty of the most heinous kind
A nation out of its collective disUnited mind
One way or another
Mourned or scorned their sisters and brothers
The thin blue line
Became the next in line
To be further maligned
BLM became as by the way as BLT
Racism endemic became
Both rally cry and plea

Statues were torn down
Monuments of history
Or a semi-fictionalised or maginalised half-forgotten
    past
'You can't obliterate all that's been!'
Said those whose own pedestal
They ungratefully perched upon
Raised on music that's the legacy of slaves' songs
While the liberal and compassionate proclaimed
    'This idolatry is wrong!'
On gadgets made with minerals
Keeping children buried in African mines
Racism, in practice, unites us all
And yet we just can't seem to get along

Meanwhile Covid 19
Remained behind and dominating all but every
    scene
The masked became two-a-penny superheroes
But once it slipped below the nose
Public enemies became
Semi-exposed in viral shame

Trump lost
Badly
He had talked of becoming tired of winning
Not so of golfing
Incarcerating infants
Or never really joking or laughing, even grinning
From fake news to a rigged election
The self-claimed finest POTUS ever
Like a pussy grabbed by an uninvited erection
Would have to move on like a bitch
At this, the bigliest
Shame-filled failed re-selection

Vaccination
Becomes an ululation
Salvation seems tangible once again
But...
Who gets it?
How long does it last for?
And how do we manage..?
Let's hope the logistics
Are handled by those more capable than SAGE
Be hopeful yet vigilant
Try not to die of respiratory failure
At the same time be careful not to hold your breath
We handed self-defeat to our cheating leaders
Let's see how we compete against untimely death

The deal is done
What was broke is brokered
A bridge across a Channel-wide breach
At the eleventh hour (and 59 seconds) reached
Like a present
From the ghost of Christmas present
The red tape
Whitewashing
And blues
Have come to...
What exactly?
An end?
An uncertain new beginning?
The future's ever uncertain
No matter whose anthem
You are, or are not, singing

The coronavirus
Or the particular coronavirus
That seems to have found fame as the one and only
Possibly scared of its human host leaving it lonely
Ate a can of spinach
And grew bulging muscles
The strengthometer stretching to tier four
London tussled
To get out of town
And dodge the stretchers heading for the morgue
Johnson crosses Xmas off the list
With a pish, we're all shut down
The former colonial empire
Becomes a leper colony
As if hexxed by Brexit
Alone, all out at sea

It's been a good year for
Amazon
Netflix
Zoom
Tinder
And Pfizer look set to make even more of a killing
Than they did when they blocked AIDS drugs to
    developing nations
And Track and Trace (who failed to keep us safe)
Stole the letters N, H and S
And pilfered billions from taxpayers
The whereabouts of which is anyone's guess

2020
Brought us together
Forced us apart
Made us realise how important our jobs are
Or aren't
A hundredfold hidden agendas that are not
Against countless barely concealed government plots
The economy was said to be in near collapse
Because people bought what they need instead of
    crap
While Bezos shipped more shit than has ever been
    previously known
No wonder we need fourteen thousand toilet rolls at
    home

We binge watched
And overate
And stayed up late
Lost track of the time and days
Queued for hours and hours
For the first time experimented with flour
Lifted unread books off dust-encrusted shelves
And laid them left unread elsewhere
Time's coveted in its absence
Once in abundance - well, who cares?
Homeschooled
Broke rules
Then, before we learned what the new rules were
Learned the likes of us was why they had occurred
Painted pictures
Composed songs
Knitted
Sewed
And oh so alone, our oats tissue sowed
Lockdown lust conceived
A C-19 generation
While isolation and online porn
Spawned mass joyless masturbation
Home officed
Wept, slept, felt overtly inept
Paired formerly estranged socks
Had conversations with our spouses
Mothballed our best purse-emptying frocks
Drank drinks like drunks

Opened up the family chest, fever-tweeted into funk
Said goodbye to those who died
Or were unable to as they did so alone
Tuned the retired into tech
(Hell, even I bought my first smartphone)
Went for walks
Listened to TED Talks
Strangers exchanged pleasantries
Partners and parents platitudes
Domestic violence soared, as were
Chins kept up to force the mood
Some did this
Some did that
Some got fed up
Some starved, some got fat
And arrogant
Opinionated
Curmudgeonly
Would be witty
Subjectively logical
Unwittingly comical
Sprawling excuses
For poetry were penned
No end

For sure, 2020 will be a long-standing meme
Preferably with the near future dramatically
    changing the theme
But if you think putting Covid behind us will save
    our skins and the day
XR may remind you nature might have something
    else to say
Why not relax with a book? Maybe one set in the
    year to come
Like P D James' *The Children of Men*
Or if that's not your idea of fun
Put on a movie set in this year, and pour yourself a
    rum
Such as *A Quiet Place*
Happy new (world order) year,
Everyone!

THE WAR

The argument for recycling
Is as watertight as our plastic bins
As we all have seen
On our lithium
Cobalt
And poison screens
Seas full of plastic
Countless creatures enmeshed
In non-degradable
Imperishable evidence
Of human degradation
An ecocidal mess
But when it comes time to empty them
Paper, plastic, glass and all
Have the general waste overflowing
I ask what is the cause
'I didn't have time
Or patience
Or whatever it was of which I was out.'
The counter-argument given weight
By the volume approaching that of a shout
'Big fucking deal. Who the fuck cares?
Maybe I was confused.'
As if my costless token effort
Was an act of domestic abuse

The air turns blue
And then 'I forgot to call...'
And a name is supplied
Of someone they normally say's a "whore"
'Reach into my bag,
Hand me my phone.'
'But you're driving,
Doing forty
In a thirty an hour zone.'
'Jesus, I'll find it myself.
Why did I bother asking?'
'Just pull over, will you?
It's my life too you're risking.'
'Look at that driver
And that driver,
They're on their phones too.
You might be Mr fucking Perfect
But don't judge others because you're you.'

I announced I would be busy
The following Saturday
She told me 'That's OK,
I've got my own thing on anyway.'
The day arrived
Without drama or applause
At its end I checked my phone
To find several missed calls
'I've fallen off a ladder
I'm all black and blue.'
'Jesus, are you OK?'
'Yes, I am, no thanks to you.'
'I told you over a week ago
I wouldn't be there.'
'You would have been with me
If you really cared.'
'Excuse me?' I spluttered
And begged her pardon
'This is the end
Of our rose garden.
My father
Would not have let my mother climb a ladder alone.'
And then the line went as dead
As my ability to ever atone

You can have the monopoly
On rationality
Have reason
Logic
And sense
On your side
Own an argument
Even win a battle
You can have a moral victory
Empathise with the best with the against
Empathise with the best with the for
But you will never
Ever ever
Against human stupidity
Never ever
Ever ever
Ever
Win the war

WHAT DID YOU JUST SAY??

Byzantium
To Constantinople
To Istanbul
Burma to Myanmar
Ayers Rock to Uluru
Siam to Thailand
Persia to Iran
Brad's Drink to Pepsi-Cola
Afghan- to Talibanistan

Salisbury to Harare
Cornwell to le Carré
Bombay to Mumbai
Eskimo to Edy's Pie
Sex change
To gender realignment
To gender reassignment
What you said
To what you say you said
To what you say you actually meant

Brontë to Bell
Evans to Eliot
Blair to Orwell
Plastic to cosmetic
Christian to first
Fat to overweight
Good to bad to sick to dope
The one we most love
To the one we most hate

Anti-Zionist
To Antisemite
Covid 19
To kung flu
Eugenicism
To centre right
Empirical evidence
To fake news
Hate speech vociferator
To free speech gladiator
The abuser
To the one
Who claims they're the abused

Colonialism
To civilisation
Tax avoidance
To wealth creation
Voice of reason
To guilty of treason
Spring, summer, fall...
To nonstop heatwave season

Slaveholder
To entrepreneur
Full time employees
To food bank poor
Illiteral
To literally
Information Age
To semi-literacy
An exhibitionistocracy
Fearful for their privacy
Whatever it was and whatever it is
To whatever us idiots say it'll be

THE WORLD THAT OUGHT TO BE

What would you say was your ideal?
What, in your version of an ideal world
However fairy tale that sounds
Would be what makes it go round?
How would you describe it?
And what, compared to the world in which you
    currently live
Would be its advantages?
What would make the version you envisage
Of more worldly benefit?

Do you like to make people happy?
Or get a buzz out of making others feel crappy?
Do you have a concept of an underdog
You'd like to put in their place?
Or seek equity for the shiny happy human race?
Is your dream in equal parts futile and noble?
Or is your fantasy one
You wouldn't like associated with your name and
    face?

I don't like people
I really, really, really, really, really don't like people
I'm sorry
If I need to apologise
Can you forgive me
For my underlying enmity?
I haven't the heart to lie
That wouldn't be nice

But the smile I wear
Is one I do not force
For if I try to force one
It looks like a fool and a coward having intercourse
I dig the passionate
The creative
The kind
And those with an open mind
A billion cold hearts
Give me the shivers
But a single warm nature
Delivers, delivers, and delivers

Do you seek revenge?
Do you want to get even?
Or uneven?
Do you want more than most?
Or to be the subject of a toast?
I'm only asking
Because the evidence suggests there are plenty who
do
And see it as something of which to boast

Do you want to exterminate
Ethnicities?
Raze entire cities?
Make the other sex your bitch?
Or make those who do not recognise
The gender you see yourself
Represent apologise
For seeing you as a glitch?
Do you seek a world that's just?
Or an outlet to justify
Your impossible to satisfy
Bloodlust?
Do you express your ideal
Through gritted teeth, with a sneer?
You'll show that fucking ex, those ragheads, kikes
and spicks and queers...

From fleeting flights of fancy
To bleats of 'Get real!'
The distance imagination takes you
Is whatever holds the most appeal
For me, the measure of a person
Is in the breadth of their ideal
Is yours closer to Guanyin
Or to Zeus' lightning bolt zeal?

Printed in Great Britain
by Amazon

31327770R00106